Strawberry Shortcake™

The Berrylicious Bake-off

A Scratch-and-Sniff STORY

Written by Monique Z. Stephens
Illustrated by SI Artists

Grosset & Dunlap • New York

Strawberry Shortcake™ © 2003 Those Characters From Cleveland, Inc. Used under license by Penguin Putnam Inc.
All rights reserved. Published by Grosset & Dunlap, a division of Penguin Putnam Books for Young Readers,
345 Hudson Street, New York, NY 10014. GROSSET & DUNLAP is a trademark of Penguin Putnam Inc.
Published simultaneously in Canada. Printed in Thailand.

ISBN 0-448-43186-6   A B C D E F G H I J

One day, Angel Cake was inside her cake shop with her pet lamb, Vanilla Icing.

"I'm bored," Angel Cake said. "Today would be a great day to do something fun with all of my berry best friends. But what should we do?"

She looked over at Vanilla Icing. But Vanilla was busy looking at the pretty three-layer cake in the display case. Vanilla loved eating Angel's cakes. And Angel loved making them.

"That's it!" Angel shouted. "I'll invite everyone over to bake a cake. It'll be the most berrylicious day ever!" She called all of her friends and got started making the cake batter.

"I can't wait to eat our yummy strawberry shortcake," Strawberry Shortcake said happily.

"But I was hoping to make an orange turnover cake!" Orange Blossom cried.

"What about a gingerbread cake?" Ginger Snap suggested. "That's always good."

"But not as good as my famous huckleberry tart," said Huckleberry Pie.

Honey Pie Pony shook her head. "Famous? My fudge brownies, that's what's famous. Why, kings and queens have eaten my delicious brownies!"

Even Apple Dumplin' held up one of the red apples she had brought. "Apple gake," she cooed.

"We can't make all of those cakes," Angel Cake cried. "My kitchen's too small!"

Then she got an idea. "But maybe there's a recipe that will make everyone happy. We'll start with these," she said, grabbing one of Orange Blossom's oranges.

The friends got busy slicing and squeezing the juicy oranges.

"We'll add the orange juice to the cake batter," said Angel Cake.

"Orange-flavored cake?" Orange Blossom asked. "Now that sounds different!"

"But delicious!" said Strawberry Shortcake.

They poured the batter into two cake pans and put them in the oven to bake.

Next, they chopped the strawberries and cooked them with sugar on the stove top to make jam.

The oven's bell timer rang. "The cake's done!" Angel Cake cried.

As soon as the cakes had cooled, Strawberry Shortcake spread the sweet strawberry jam on the bottom cake layer.

"Strawberry filling!" said Huckleberry Pie. "What a great idea!"

"The next part's easy," said Angel Cake. She whispered something in Ginger Snap's ear. Ginger Snap smiled. She grabbed her gingersnap cookies and put them on top of the strawberry filling. "Ta da! A yummy crispy cookie layer!"

Then Angel Cake put the second cake on top of the cookies and covered it with strawberry jam, too.

"Your huckleberries are next, Huckleberry Pie," she said.

"All right!" Huckleberry cheered.

"And now we're finally ready for Honey Pie Pony's delicious fudge," said Angel Cake. "Fudge makes a great topping!"

"You're amazing, Angel Cake!" Strawberry cried. "With your help, we've made the berry best cake ever—and we even used everyone's favorite ingredients!"

"Uh-oh," said Orange Blossom. "Not everyone's. We forgot about Apple Dumplin's apples!"

Angel Cake laughed. "Oh, I didn't forget. We can use them to make apple juice! We can't eat cake without something to drink, can we?"

"This is the berry best cake I've ever had," said Huckleberry.

"Me too," said Ginger Snap. "Who would have thought so many berry different ingredients could make one berry perfect cake?"

The friends raised their cups in a toast. "Here's to Angel Cake!" said Strawberry Shortcake. "And her most berrylicious recipe ever!